Tucker
and the
Special Baseball

by Dale Lundberg
illustrated by Kevin Rechin

SCHOOL PUBLISHERS

Printed in China

ISBN 10: 0-15-351533-3
ISBN 13: 978-0-15-351533-0

Ordering Options
ISBN 10: 0-15-351214-8 (Grade 4 Advanced Collection)
ISBN 13: 978-0-15-351214-8 (Grade 4 Advanced Collection)
ISBN 10: 0-15-358123-9 (package of 5)
ISBN 13: 978-0-15-358123-6 (package of 5)

4 5 6 7 8 9 10 0940 12 11 10 09

Tucker Bradley was having a bad day. In fact, he was having a bad summer. His baseball team had just lost another game, and that left the Wolverines without a single win this summer.

As Tucker sat on his front stoop, he thought about the game. The other team had been relentless, hitting ball after ball. Tucker winced as he thought about the crowd where the kids had booed him. "I don't blame them because I just wasn't any good today," he thought. It was going to be an extremely long summer.

Tucker wandered into his backyard and passed by the tree stump where he practiced pitching balls. He would set up cans on the stump and try to knock them off. As Tucker shuffled along, he noticed a baseball lying on the ground.

"Rotten baseball," he thought. Tucker tripped, and he inadvertently kicked the ball. Then a funny thing happened. The ball spun and twirled through the air. It swerved right, then left, then it sunk down and flew straight at some cans on the tree stump. WHACK! The cans went flying. Tucker stared at the baseball, his mouth open in amazement. He went over to the baseball and slowly picked it up. Then he set the cans back up on the stump and backed away.

He stood, took aim, and pitched. The ball zipped and curved through the air. Tucker had thrown the ball too high, but it sank low at the last second. POW! Again, the cans flew off the stump.

Tucker just stared at the ball for a few moments. He looked around to see whether anyone else was witnessing what he was seeing. Then he picked up the baseball and pitched it over and over again. No matter how poorly he pitched, the ball always zipped around and then knocked the cans right off of the stump!

Tucker's heart began to pound. There was something wonderfully strange about this baseball. It was obviously a very special ball. Tucker stuffed it in his pocket, went into his house, and for the first time that day, he actually smiled.

The following Friday, Tucker could hardly wait to show up at the field. His friend Axle was running in the field trying to catch fly balls. Benjamin was practicing his slides into second base. The other players took turns throwing and batting.

Tucker saw Midori, the only girl on the team, coming toward him. He groaned. None of the boys objected to having her on the team, but the truth was that she was better than most of them. Midori was from Japan, and she had just learned English. Her teacher must have given her special lessons on how to bother Tucker.

"Hey, Tucker," said Midori, "are you pitching today?"

"Yes, Midori, what about it?" replied Tucker.

"Hope you do better today," Midori smiled. She really did have good intentions, but she really did bother Tucker.

Tucker smiled to himself. He wasn't going to give Midori a reason to bother him today. He reached inside his pocket and felt the special baseball. Today the Wolverines would win.

As Tucker walked onto the field, Coach Cantor called out to the team. No matter how poorly they played, Coach Cantor always gave them great pep talks.

"Today we're playing the Bears. They have the best record in the league, so let's go out there and show these guys how you play ball. Remember, it's how you play the game that counts," the coach said.

The team put their hands together and gave a whooping cheer. Tucker cheered with his teammates. Once again, he felt the special baseball in his pocket, and he knew for sure that today his team would win.

Tucker stepped up to the mound with Reynolds Ray up at bat. He was the best hitter for the Bears. "Come on, Bradley, let's see what you've got," Reynolds taunted.

Tucker would not let his anger be roused by Reynolds. He curled his fingers around his special baseball. He stood up straight, aimed, and dealt the pitch. The ball zipped left, then right, and swooshed right by Reynolds.

"Strike one!" called the umpire.

Tucker wound up for the second pitch. The special ball zigzagged through the air and then dipped low for a sinker.

"Strike two!" shouted the umpire.

Tucker's third pitch blew right by Reynolds, who appeared to be in a state of shock. "You're out!" yelled the umpire.

Reynolds stared at Tucker, who smiled right back at him. This was going to be a good day. Reynolds walked away, shaking his head. This could not possibly be happening because Tucker was the worst pitcher in the league.

For the next three innings, the special ball zipped, dipped, and curved past each batter at the plate. No matter how Tucker threw the baseball, it always flew straight over the plate. The batters swung wildly at the pitches and Tucker struck them all out. The crowd was on its feet, cheering loudly, while Tucker's stature grew taller with each strike.

Then something terrible happened! Tucker wound up for the pitch and threw the ball. The baseball zipped right past the batter, the catcher, and the umpire. To Tucker's surprise, the ball kept going and disappeared under the snack stand.

The umpire tossed a new ball to Tucker. "Now what will I do?" Tucker panicked. He dealt the pitch, and the batter swung. CRACK! Up and away went the ball. The batter made it to second base, and the next batter stood at the plate. WHACK! The ball flew past right field, good for a home run.

Batter after batter hit the ball. Before Tucker and his team knew it, the Bears were up by six runs, and there was only one more inning to go.

Tucker was a resourceful boy and he was not about to let a chance to win the game pass him by. He looked around him and then headed off to the snack stand where the ball had rolled.

Tucker quickly crawled under the snack stand where
his special ball was lying. As he reached for it, he suddenly
remembered what his coach had said: "It's how you play
the game that counts."

He thought, "If I use this ball, I'm cheating." He stared
at the ball for a moment and knew how sad his family
would be if they found out he had not been honest. Then
he thought, "If I am going to win this game, it's not going
to be with the help of this silly ball! I'm going to
win this game by myself!" Tucker took one last look at
the ball, and then he looked out at the vast crowd. "I don't
care if I get booed, either."

As Tucker walked back to the bench, the Wolverines were up at bat. Then a strange thing happened. Tucker Bradley's teammates actually began to *hit* the ball! Midori stood at the plate and clocked one into right field, while Axle boomed one to center. Before they knew it, the Wolverines had scored seven runs and had taken the lead!

Now it was time for Tucker to pitch. If the Bears did not score, the Wolverines would win the game. He stepped up to the mound as the crowd roared. Tucker wound up and pitched to the batter. "I don't need any special baseballs," he thought. "I can do this all on my own."

"Strike!" called the umpire. Tucker threw again—another strike. One more pitch, and this time, it was strike three.

There were two more outs to go and another batter stepped up to the plate. Tucker dealt, one, two, three strikes for the second out. Then the last player, Reynolds Ray, stepped up to the plate. Tucker thought, "If I can get him out, we win."

Tucker wound up and pitched. The first two balls sailed right past Reynolds for strikes. "One more strike," thought Tucker as he threw the ball.

Reynolds swung and hit the ball. The ball flew into the air, and Tucker stopped breathing, but there was his friend Axle, running for the catch. Axle reached for the ball and tumbled in a heap. Tucker couldn't bear to look but then he heard the crowd cheering. When he opened his eyes, there was Axle, holding up the ball. The Wolverines had actually won!

Midori, Benjamin, Coach Cantor, Axle, and the other players all rushed to the pitcher's mound. The whole team joined in the celebration and they jumped wildly in the air. Tucker received bountiful compliments from his teammates.

"Tucker, what a great game you pitched!" yelled Midori.

"You did a pretty good job yourself!" Tucker replied. The two teammates slapped each other high fives. Axle and Benjamin were jumping up and down, hugging each other.

Now it was time for the coach's pep talk. "I am so proud of the way you all played the game," he said.

Tucker beamed as his teammates cheered, because he was so happy at that moment. Something strange and wonderful had happened that day, but in the end, Tucker and his team had done it on their own.

Think Critically

1. What parts of this story are fantasy?

2. How did Tucker change during the story? Explain your answer.

3. What lesson do you think the author wanted readers to learn from this story?

4. When did you first begin to think that the Wolverines might win the ball game?

5. Did Tucker make a good choice when he decided not to use the special baseball? Explain your answer.

⭐ Language Arts

Write an Article Pretend you are a sports reporter for Tucker's local newspaper. Write an article about the game between the Wolverines and the Bears.

 Home-School Connection Ask family or friends whether they ever played team sports. Discuss what sports they played. See whether they can remember their most dramatic moments.

Word Count: 1,530